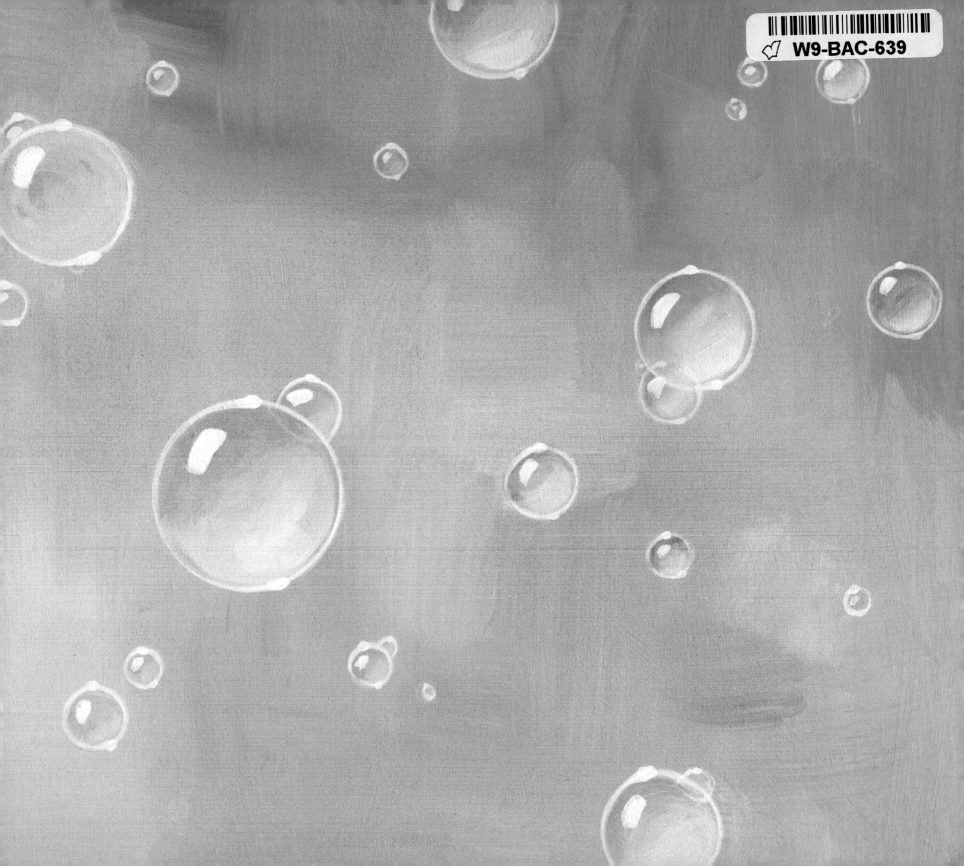

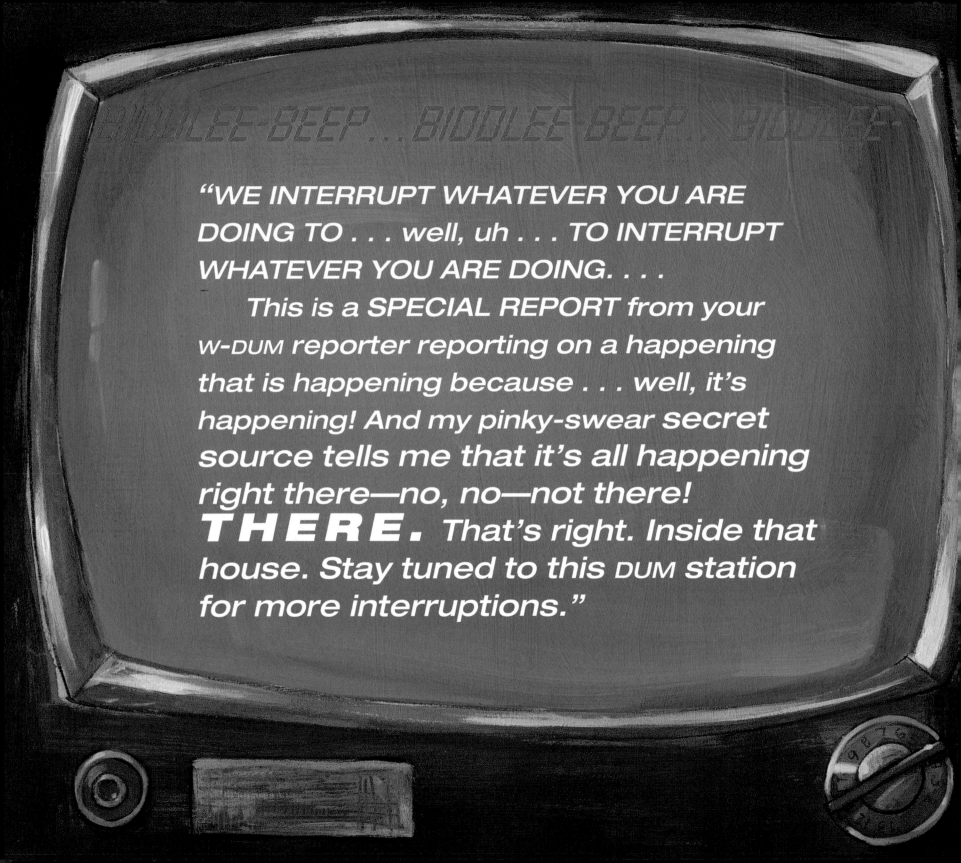

BIDDLEE-BEEP . . . BIDDLEE-BEEP . . . BIDDLEE-

"WE INTERRUPT WHATEVER YOU ARE DOING TO . . . well, uh . . . TO INTERRUPT WHATEVER YOU ARE DOING. . . .

This is a SPECIAL REPORT from your W-DUM reporter reporting on a happening that is happening because . . . well, it's happening! And my pinky-swear secret source tells me that it's all happening right there—no, no—not there! **THERE.** *That's right. Inside that house. Stay tuned to this DUM station for more interruptions."*

tub-boo-boo

by Margie Palatini
illustrated by Glin Dibley

Simon & Schuster Books for Young Readers
New York   London   Toronto   Sydney   Singapore

Sources, schmources. Puh-lease.

If you want to know the real inside stuff, trust ME, Lucy Hathaway. How do I know all the inside stuff? Because I'm inside. I mean, I live inside. I mean, THAT house is MY house. . . .

Let's see now . . . where should I begin? The beginning is always a good place. Which was when my little brother, Henry, walked through the back door this afternoon at exactly 4:15 P.M.

"You're filthy," said Mother to Henry.

"Where?" said Henry to Mother.

"Here. There. Everywhere," said Mother. "Now march yourself right up those stairs, young man, and take a bath."

"A bath? In the middle of the day?" Henry groaned, but hep-two'd, then turned. "Water up to my chin?"

"Knees," said Mother.

"Elbows," said Henry, "AND with bubbles."

Mother sighed. "Deal."

Henry smiled. "Done."

Negotiations completed, they shook hands and headed for the tub.

The drain got plugged, the spout spurted water, and Mother dripped a drop of Double Bubble Bubble Bath. One drop. One measly little drip of a drop. Now, everybody knows that one little measly drip of a drop doesn't make a respectable tubful of bubbles. Everyone knows that. Even a little squirt like Henry.

So . . . Henry just squirted in a little extra—well, a little more than a little extra. Okay. A lot more than a little extra. He poured in the whole bottle of Double Bubble Bubble Bath.

Boy. That label didn't lie. The bubble juice brewed and bubbled—up. Up. Up. Higher. Higher. So much higher that Mother lost sight of the squirt, spout, and everything else in the tub.

"Henry? Henry? Oh, Henry? Where are you, Henry?"

"Here," answered a voice from somewhere inside the soapy suds.

POOF.

PUFF.

PPPFF.

"Right here," Henry said, blowing a hole through a high drift and poking out his head.

Mother was relieved to know that Henry was safe, sound—and clean. And Henry continued to splish, splash, and snorkel his way to a dirt-free epidermis.

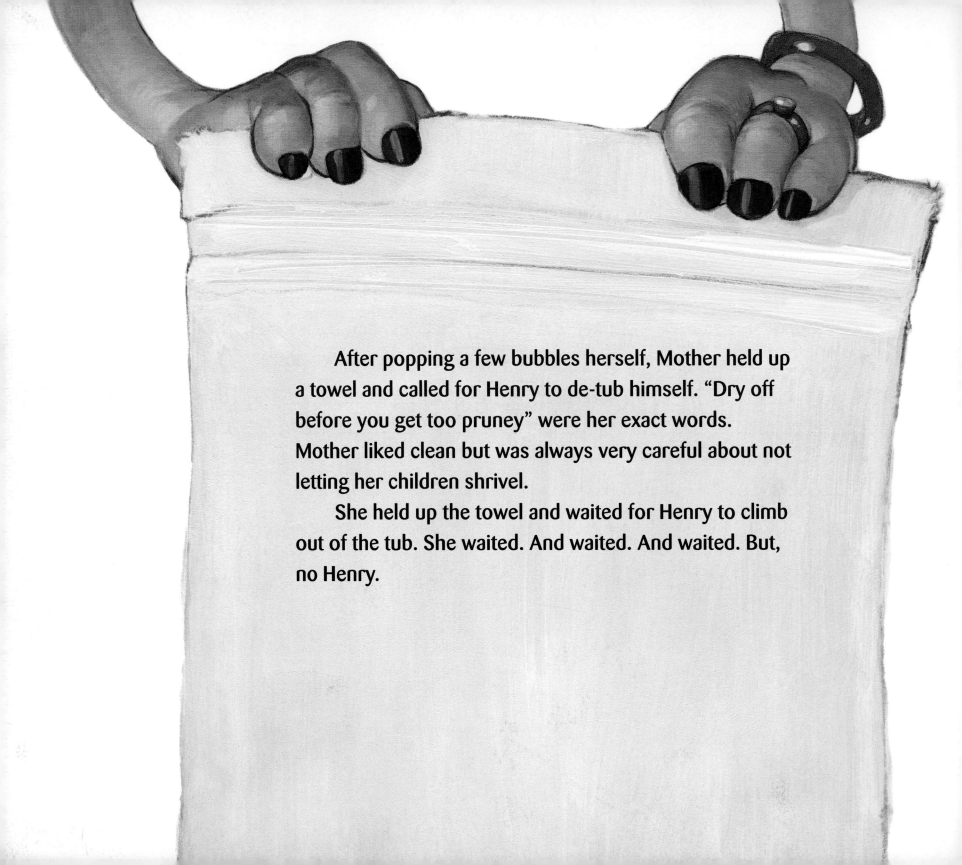

After popping a few bubbles herself, Mother held up a towel and called for Henry to de-tub himself. "Dry off before you get too pruney" were her exact words. Mother liked clean but was always very careful about not letting her children shrivel.

She held up the towel and waited for Henry to climb out of the tub. She waited. And waited. And waited. But, no Henry.

"Oops."

"What oops?" said Mother.

"Big oops," said Henry. "I think I made a boo-boo . . . a TUB-boo-boo."

"A tub-what-who?"

"A tub-boo-boo. I just wanted to stop one drippy drop. Slow the flow with my little big toe. And now—I'm stuck! I'm stuck in the tub and can't get out."

"Impossible," said Mother, shoving a mountain of bubbles this way and scooping a billow of bubbles that way.

But it wasn't impossible. It was very, very possible. He was stuck, all right. Henry's little big toe was stuck smack-dab right up inside the spout where the water was supposed to spit and spurt.

Mother, being Mother, kicked off her shoes, pulled off her socks, rolled up her pants, and jumped in feet first to try to free Henry. She squatted. Then squinted. Of course, Mother knew just what to do. She was absolutely sure, positively positive that if she could just wiggle her fingers up into the spigot and wrangle them around Henry's little big toe . . . why . . . well . . . uh . . .

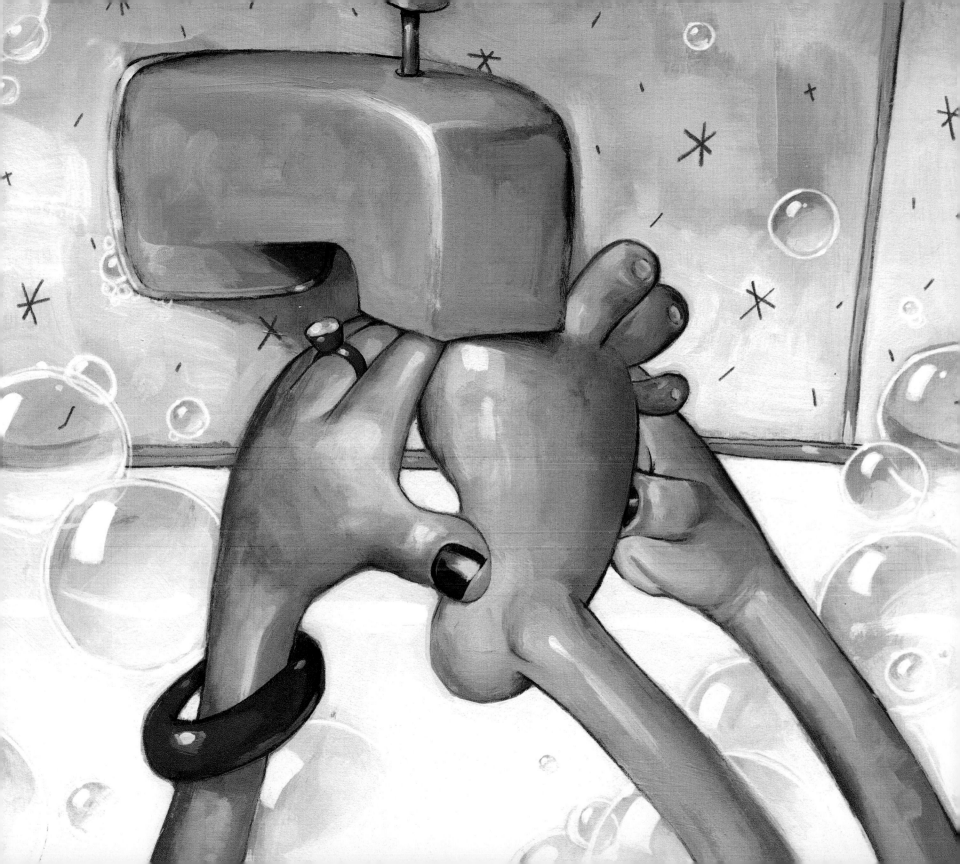

"Oops."

"What oops?" said Henry.

"Big oops," said Mother. "I think I made a tub-boo-boo."

So there they were. The two of them stuck in the tub. Mother squinting and squatting with her fingers squished up inside the spigot against Henry's little big toe, which was stuck smack-dab in the spout where the water was supposed to spit and spurt. Oh yes, they pulled. They yanked. They were stuck, all right.

"HELP! HELP! HELP!"

"What the hay?" said Dad, seeing the two in the tub.

"We made a tub-boo-boo," said Henry and Mother.

"A tub-what-who?" said Dad.

"A tub-boo-boo! Tub-boo-boo. We're stuck in the tub and can't get out!"

"Impossible!" said Dad.

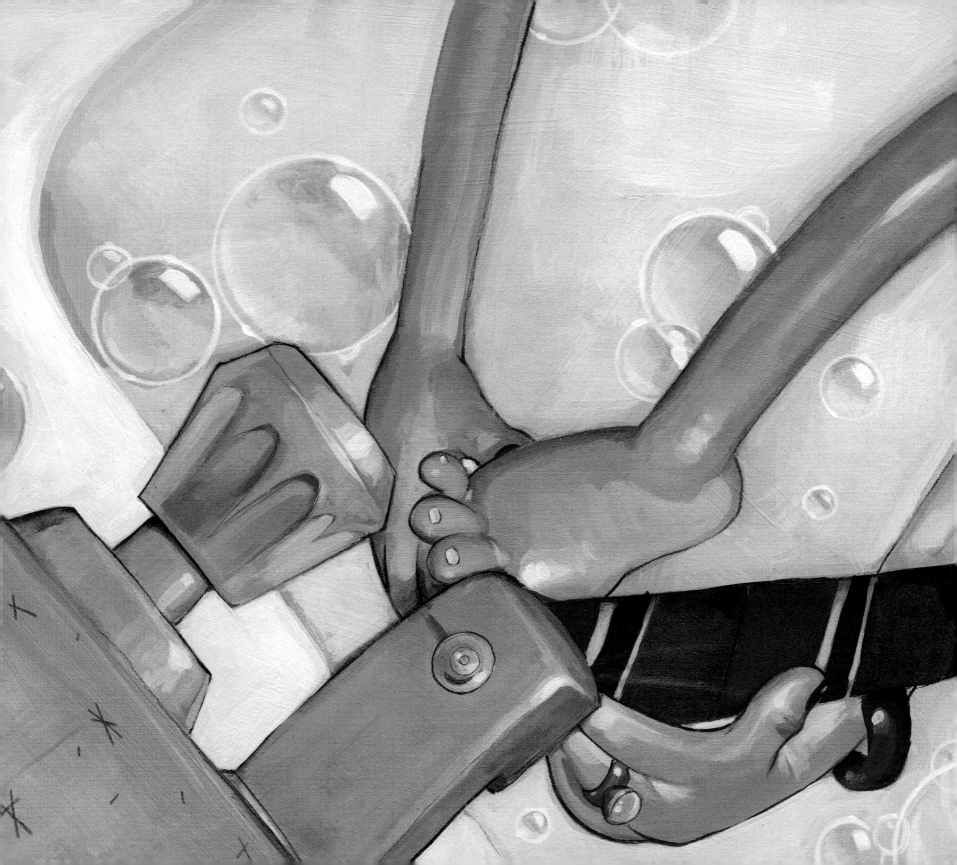

Dad, being Dad, dove right in with a splish and a splash, straddled the suds, and bravely battled the bubbles to free Henry and Mother. Of course, Dad knew just what to do. He was absolutely sure, positively positive that if he could just squish his tie up into the spigot and lasso it around Mother's fingers, which were wrangled around Henry's little big toe . . . why . . . well . . . uh . . .

"Oops."

"What oops?" said Henry and Mother.

"Big oops," said Dad. "I think I made a tub-boo-boo."

So there they were. The three of them stuck in the tub. Dad straddling and battling with his tie pushed up into the spigot right next to Mother's fingers, which were squished up against Henry's little big toe, which was stuck smack-dab in the spout where the water was supposed to spit and spurt. Yes-sir-ee. They were stuck.

But—aha! Dad had his PHONE. So Mother picked his pocket, and Henry beeped the buttons, and they all shouted, "Help! Help! Help! Come quick! There's been a terrible tub-boo-boo!"

With lights spinning, sirens wailing, and walkie-talkie in tow, Officer Sidney R. Ottley arrived on the scene.

"POLICE! FREEZE!" he ordered, running into the bathroom.

Sidney blushed. "Oh. Excuse me," he said, turning to leave.

"NO! NO!" the three shouted. "It's a tub-boo-boo!"

"A tub-what-who?"

"A tub-boo-boo! Tub-boo-boo! We're stuck in the tub and can't get out!"

"Impossible!" said Sidney.

The policeman, being a policeman, jumped right into the tub, uniform, badge, and all, to try to free Dad, Mother, and Henry. He was absolutely sure, positively positive that he could get them out of that spout if he could just push his big little finger up and around and . . . why . . . well . . . uh . . .

"Oops."

"What oops?" said Henry, Mother, Dad.

"Big oops," said Officer Ottley. "I think I made a . . ."

"We know. We know," they sighed.

So Officer Ottley did what any grime fighter would do in a situation like this. He called in a plumber.

Then they waited. And waited. And waited. And finally the plumber arrived.

He looked. He nodded. He took out his wrench. "Ooohh, sure," he said. "One of them tub-boo-boos. I'll have you folks out of that tub in a minute."

And he did.

He got the whole spigot right out of the tub. He just didn't get them out of the spigot.

"Now what?" Mom, Dad, and Officer Ottley moaned, getting a little bent out of shape.

"Yes. Now what?" said Henry as the bubbles dwindled to a precious few. It was getting downright embarrassing.

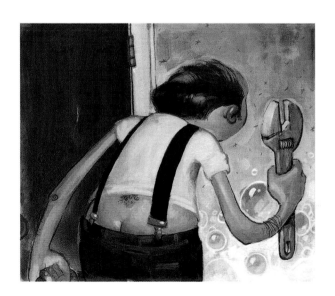

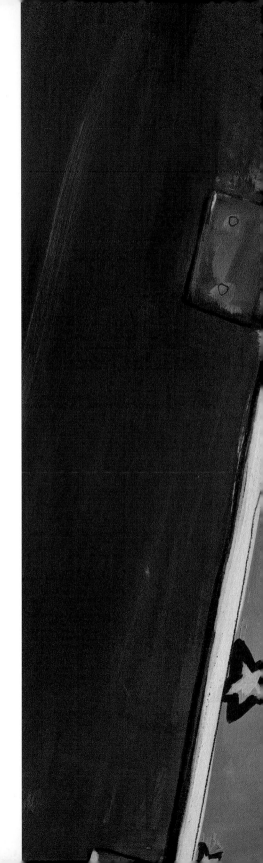

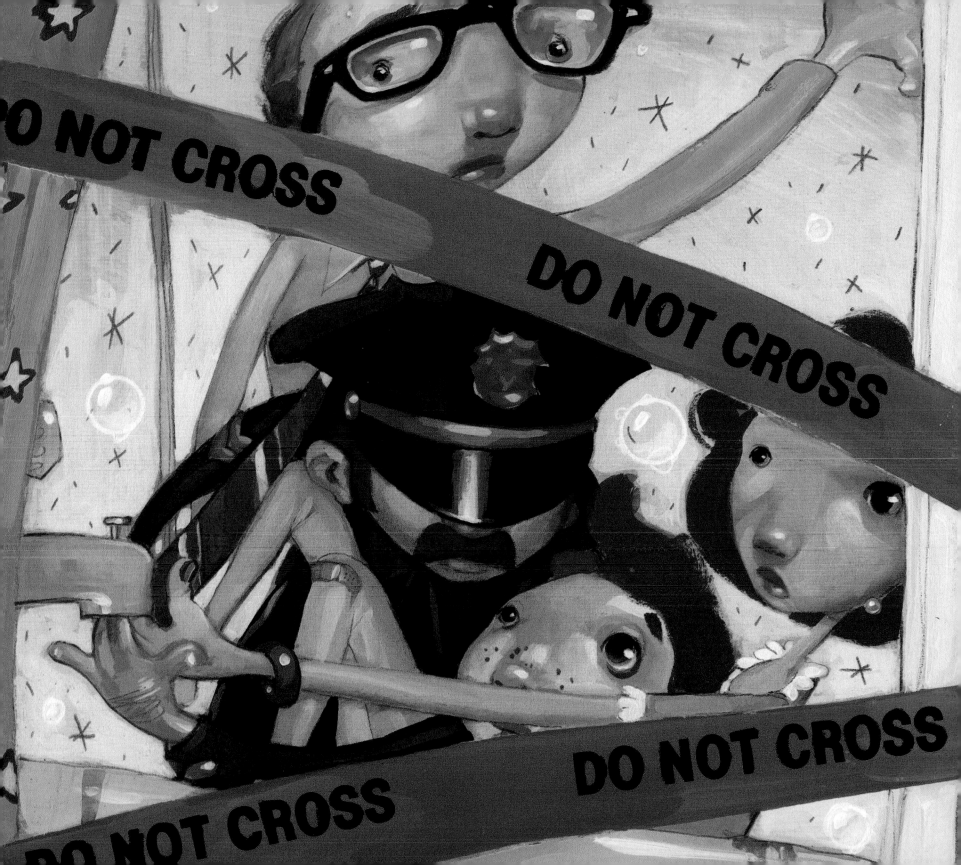

(Now, this is the part where I come in.)

"How about some ice cream?" I said, walking into the bathroom with my double-dip Chocolate Chunky Chip sugar cone.

"Lucy Hathaway! Ice cream at a time like this?" Mother screamed. Dad screamed. Henry screamed. They all screamed.

"Exactly at a time like this," I answered calmly, walking over and—ta-da! dumping the scoops into the open end of the spigot.

"Oooooh! Eeeee! Ooooh! Ahh! Ahh!"

It was cold. It was slippery. It was working!

Thlurp! First came freedom for Officer Ottley's big little finger. Shlurp! Out slid Dad's tie. Thwamp! Out came Mother's fingers. And then,

TH-TH-TH-THUWUNK!

There it was. The toe. Henry's little big toe—free, clear, and seeing daylight. It was so long, farewell, and bye-bye to the you-know-what-who.

"And just in the nick of time, too," said Henry, grabbing a towel.

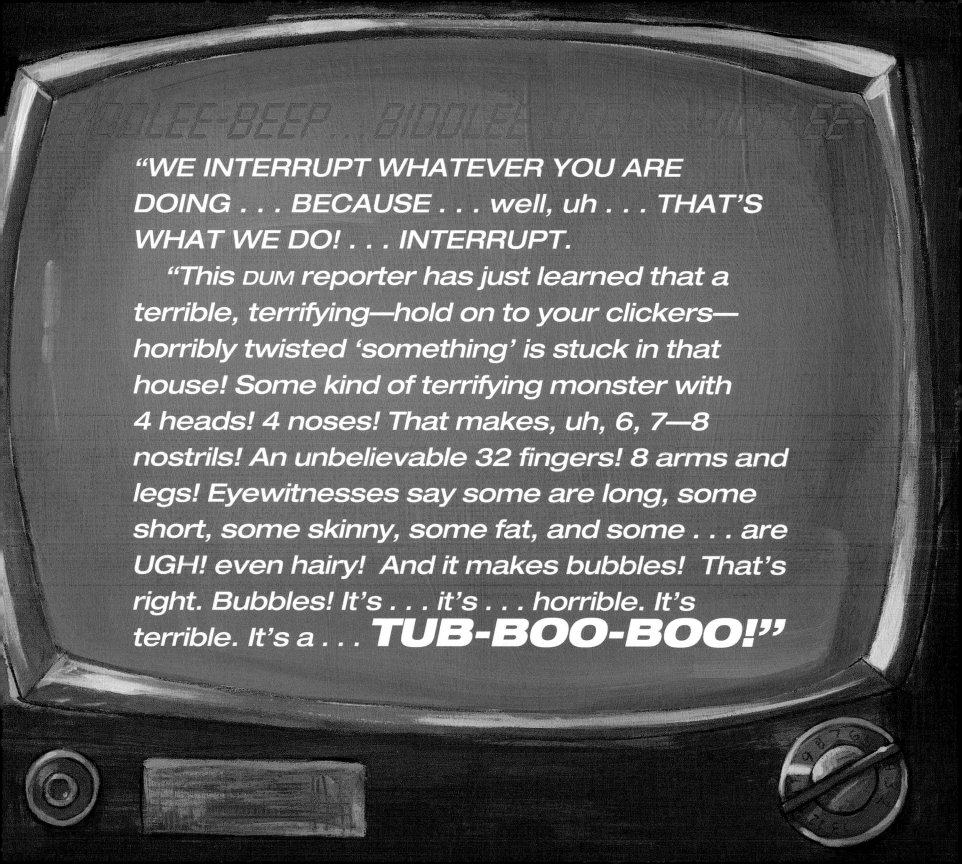

"WE INTERRUPT WHATEVER YOU ARE DOING . . . BECAUSE . . . well, uh . . . THAT'S WHAT WE DO! . . . INTERRUPT.

"This DUM reporter has just learned that a terrible, terrifying—hold on to your clickers— horribly twisted 'something' is stuck in that house! Some kind of terrifying monster with 4 heads! 4 noses! That makes, uh, 6, 7—8 nostrils! An unbelievable 32 fingers! 8 arms and legs! Eyewitnesses say some are long, some short, some skinny, some fat, and some . . . are UGH! even hairy! And it makes bubbles! That's right. Bubbles! It's . . . it's . . . horrible. It's terrible. It's a . . . **TUB-BOO-BOO!**"

Tub-what-who?

Oh, brother. What a story!
Now aren't you glad you got the
real scoop?

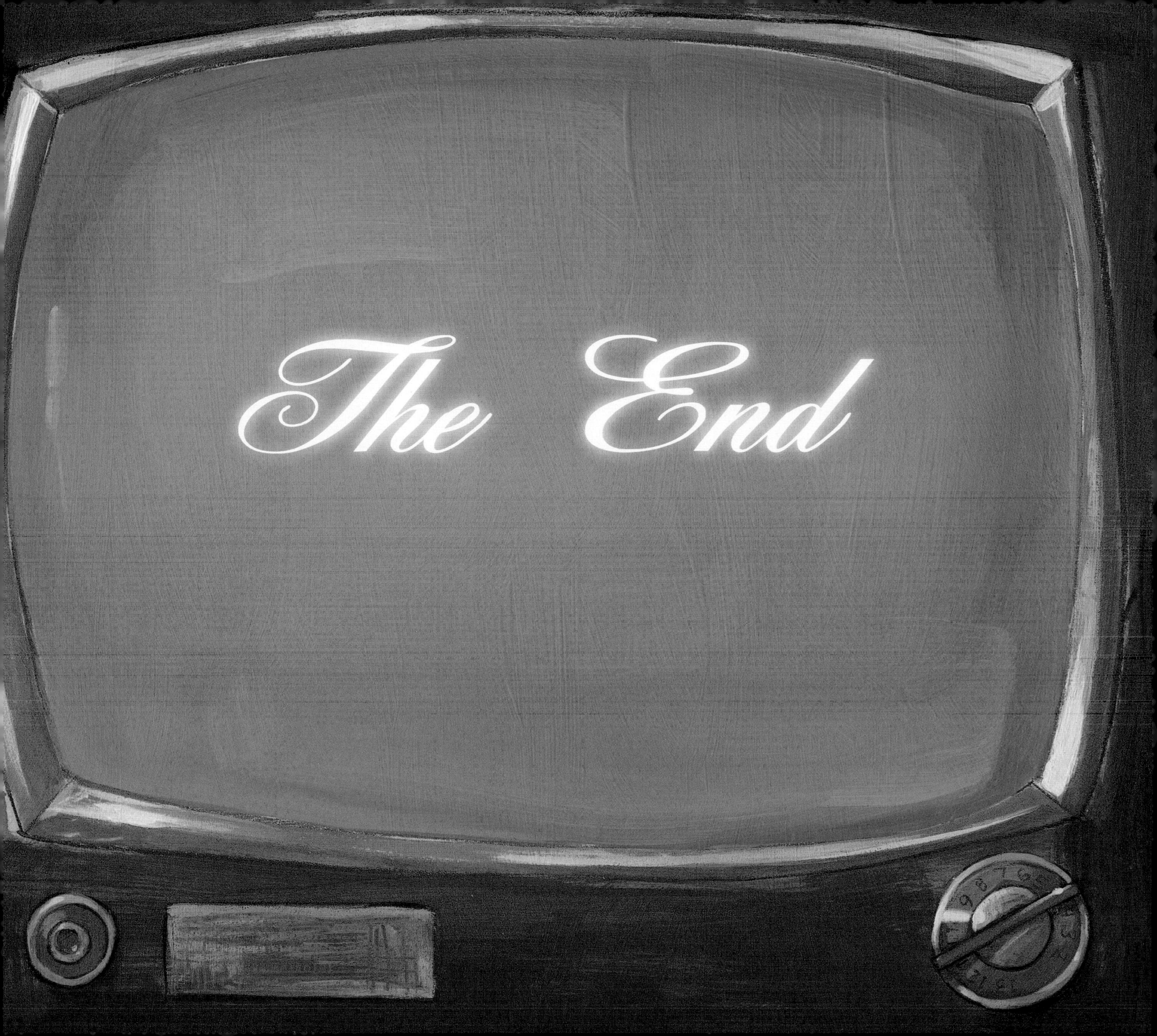
The End

In memory of Kate and Mickey, two terrific grandparents
—M. P.

To Patrick Faricy, who since school has seen all my personalities
and through thick and thin has always encouraged, challenged,
inspired, and most of all, supported me
—G. D.

SIMON & SCHUSTER BOOKS FOR YOUNG READERS
An imprint of Simon & Schuster Children's Publishing Division
1230 Avenue of the Americas, New York, New York 10020
Text copyright © 2001 by Margie Palatini
Illustrations copyright © 2001 by Glin Dibley

Book design by Anahid Hamparian
The text of this book is set in 16-point Barmeno.
The illustrations are rendered in acrylic and colored pencil.
Printed in Hong Kong
2 4 6 8 10 9 7 5 3 1

Library of Congress Cataloging-in-Publication Data
Tub-boo-boo / by Margie Palatini ; illustrated by Glin Dibley.
p. cm.
Summary: Henry gets his toe stuck in the tub spout while taking
a bath, and everyone who tries to free him gets stuck as well.
ISBN 0-689-82394-0
[1. Baths—Fiction.] I. Dibley, Glin, ill. II. Title.
PZ7.P1755 Tu 2001 [E]—dc21 99-39434